This igloo book belongs to:

....

Published in 2019
by Igloo Books Ltd
Cottage Farm
Sywell
NN6 0BJ
www.igloobooks.com

1019 002.01
2 4 6 8 10 9 7 5 3
ISBN: 978-1-78905-186-5

Written by Melanie Joyce
Illustrated by Annabel Spencely

Designed by Justine Ablett

Printed and manufactured in China

Christmas Magic

igloobooks

I'm bursting to tell you about Christmas and why it's so much fun.

It's the sparkliest, jingliest time of year and I can't wait for it to come.

Daddy will get the Christmas tree and put it up in the hall.

I'll cover it with fairy lights and sparkly glittering balls.

I'll write my note to Santa, but I always change my mind.

I'm sure Santa won't be cross though. I think he's very kind.

Carol singers will ring the bell and sing outside our door.

When they've sung their songs, I'll ask, "Can you sing some more?"

There'll be Christmas cards to all my friends, stuck with glitter and glue.

Look out when the postman comes, there might be one for you!

I'll throw snowballs at my brother, they'll go whoosh and thud and splat!

We'll laugh and make a snowman and he'll wear my Daddy's hat.

Mum will read me stories and tell tales of Christmas past.

Then when the fire goes out, it will be time for bed at last.

I'll put on my special pajamas, the ones that are white and red.

Then I'll hang my Christmas stocking at the bottom of my bed.

When I'm fast asleep, Santa will fly to visit me.

He'll wriggle down the chimney and leave presents under the tree.

I won't sleep because I'll be so excited. Christmas is loads of fun.

In the morning, I'll run downstairs and shout, "Merry Christmas, everyone!"

Happy Christmas!